Bedtime

by Nechama Dina Adelman
illustrated by Fayge Devorah Blau

Hachai
PUBLISHING

In honor of the
birth of our daughter

בתשבע צייטקא

Mendy and Seema Gansburg

✳   ✳   ✳

BEDTIME

For Alizah who doesn't let me sleep, Brochie who tries to make me,
and Ma, Ta and the gang for not commenting.
Oh, and Laila Tov ECC! N.D.A.

For my mother and our own dear Dovid F.D.B.

First Edition – Elul 5763 / September 2003
Copyright © 2003 by **HACHAI PUBLISHING**
ALL RIGHTS RESERVED

Editor: Devorah Leah Rosenfeld
Layout: Eli Chaikin

ISBN: 1-929628-12-9
LCCN: 2003103374

HACHAI PUBLISHING
Brooklyn, New York
Tel: 718-633-0100 Fax: 718-633-0103
info@hachai.com   www.hachai.com

Printed in China

Glossary

Bracha Blessing
Hashem G-d
Mezuza Parchment scroll inscribed with hand-written text of Shema, affixed to the doorposts of a Jewish home or building
Shema The "Hear O Israel" prayer

"Bedtime, Dovid,"
said Mommy.

After he brushed his
teeth and washed his
face, Mommy helped
Dovid reach high to kiss
the mezuza.

Dovid said Shema, and let Mommy tuck him in.
Then Mommy sang him his good night song.

"Lie down on your pillow,
    And snuggle up so tight.
    Close your eyes and sleep,
    It's time to say good night.

"I love you, Dovid," Mommy said. She left the door
open just a crack, so the room wouldn't be too dark.

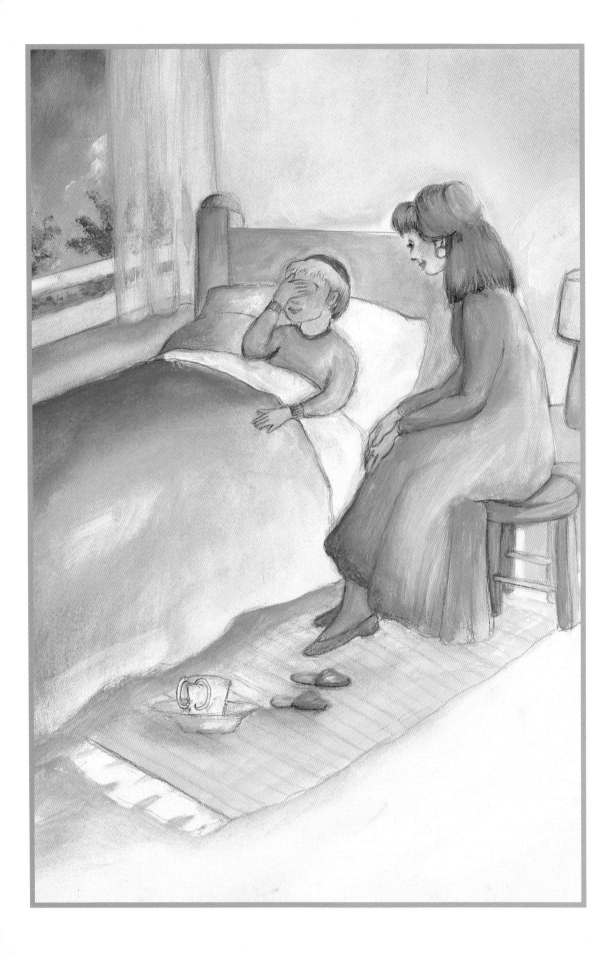

Dovid could hear her
washing dishes in the sink.
He listened to the splish, splash
of the water. He heard the plink, plink
of the plates being put in the drainer.

Then Mommy was finished.
Dovid listened, but it was quiet...
too quiet.
Dovid felt lonely.

"Mommy,"
he called.

Mommy came into
the room.
"What do you want,
Dovid?"
she asked.

Dovid thought about
the sound of the water
splashing in the sink.

"Please may I have a
drink of water?"

Mommy brought Dovid a glass of cold water, and waited as he said the bracha and drank it up.

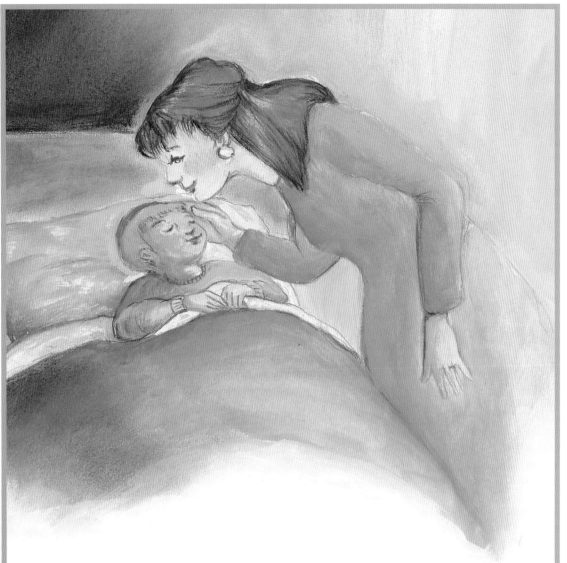

Then she sang him his good night song again.

"Lie down on your pillow,
 And snuggle up so tight.
 Close your eyes and sleep,
 It's time to say good night."

Mommy kissed Dovid on the forehead
before she left the room.

Dovid could hear
Mommy turn on the
mixer in the kitchen.
mmmm... the hum of the
mixer sounded like a noisy car.
He thought of its shiny beaters
spinning around like two shiny wheels.

Then Mommy turned it off,
and the house was quiet... too quiet.
Dovid felt lonely.

"Mommy,"
  he called.

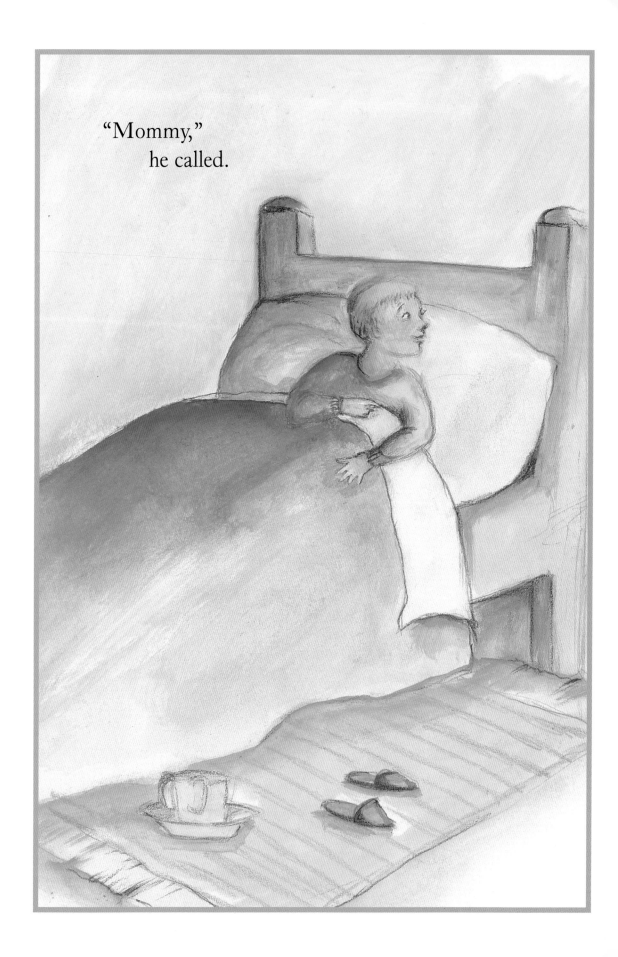

Mommy came
into the room.
"What now, Dovid?"
she asked.

Dovid thought
about the sound
of the mixer
humming like a car.

"Please may I
sleep with my car
tonight?"

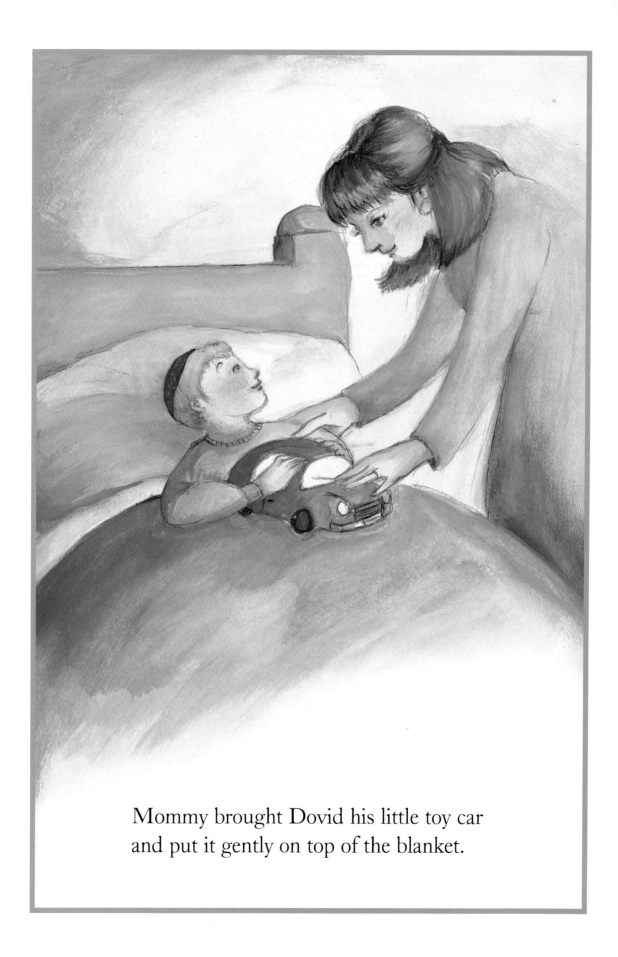

Mommy brought Dovid his little toy car
and put it gently on top of the blanket.

She sat at the end of the bed and sang,

"Lie down on your pillow,
And snuggle up so tight.
Close your eyes and sleep,
It's time to say good night."

Mommy gave Dovid a big hug before
she left the room.

Dovid could hear Mommy talking on the telephone in the living room. He liked listening to her voice get LOUDER and SOFTER, higher and lower, as she talked.

"Mommy," he called.

Mommy tiptoed in. "What's the matter, Dovid?" she asked.

Dovid thought of the nice sound of Mommy's voice. "Please will you sing the bedtime song one more time?"

Mommy sat down on Dovid's bed.
"I don't think you really need a drink
of water, your toy car, or one more song,"
she said. "I think you are just feeling lonely."

Dovid was surprised. "How did you know that?"

Mommy held Dovid's hand.
"Everyone feels lonely sometimes,
but we're never really alone.

Do you know
Who is always with us?"
Dovid knew. "Hashem," he answered.

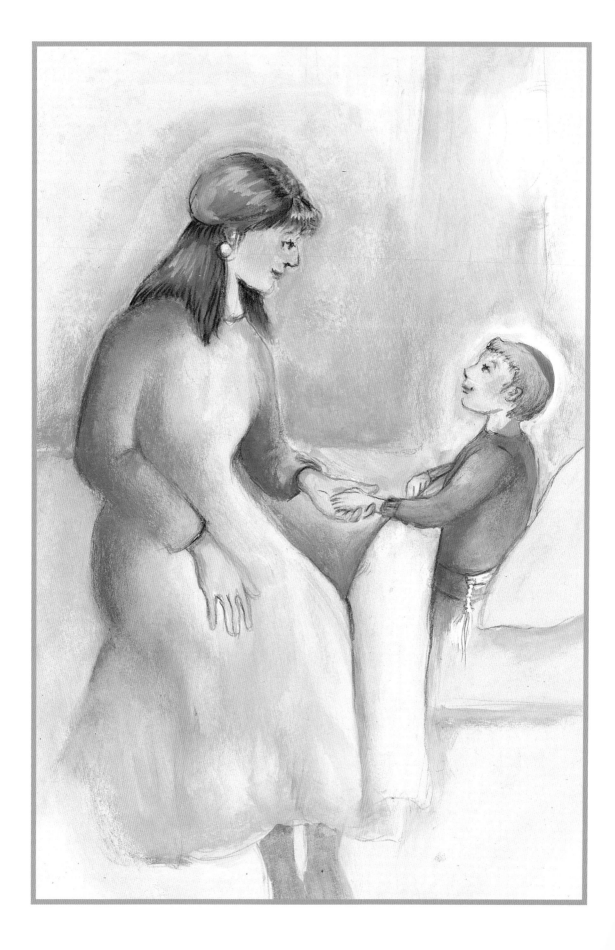

"You're right," said Mommy.
"Maybe that should be in our bedtime song."

So Mommy sang:

    "Lie down on your pillow,
      And snuggle up so tight.
      Hashem is always with you,
      It's time to say good night."

Mommy gave Dovid's hand
a squeeze and quietly
left the room.

Dovid could hear the **click, click** of her shoes as she walked down the hall. Then the house was quiet... very quiet.

Dovid wanted to call for Mommy, but he didn't.

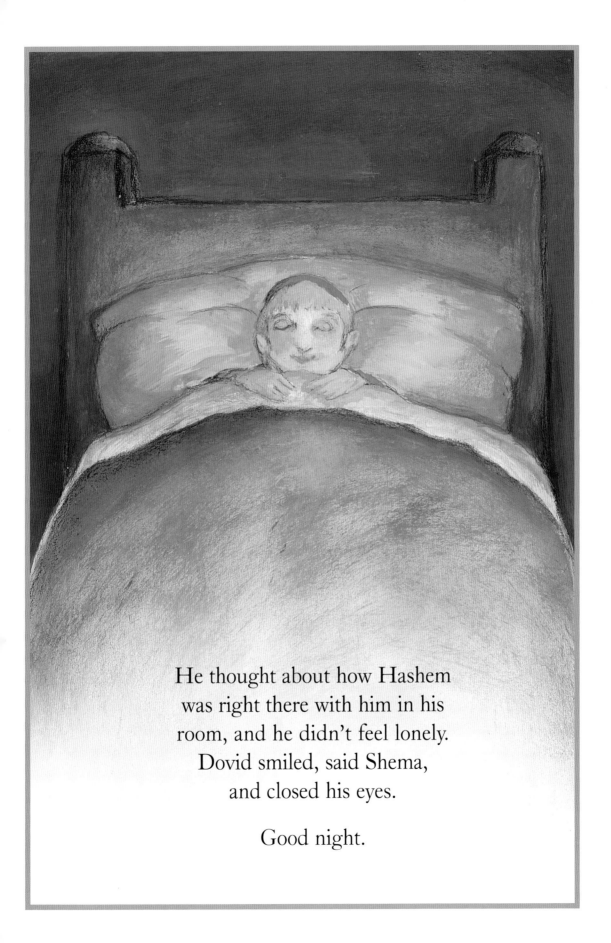

He thought about how Hashem
was right there with him in his
room, and he didn't feel lonely.
Dovid smiled, said Shema,
and closed his eyes.

Good night.

א גוטע נאכט

Cnokou Hou Houu

Bonne Nuit

לילה טוב

Good Night

Buona Notte

Buenas Noches